Dedicated to my feline friend, Amos.

Born on December 5th in a picturesque, coastal Maryland town with a French name – Havre de Grace to be exact – the small city played host to fractions fighting in The Revolutionary War. The pen name Adam Dust was developed. Twin areas of interest have been writing and filmmaking. This led to bit appearances in local, low budget films such as *Trailer Park of the Livin' Dead* as a zombie and *Mortal* as a vampire. Such creatures fuel his imagination in dark fantasy books. Under his birth name of W. P. Rigler, he has self-published the following anthologies – *Summoned Secrets* and *Midnight Writings*.

Adam Dust

THE MIDNIGHT MANSION

AUSTIN MACAULEY PUBLISHERS™

LONDON • CAMBRIDGE • NEW YORK • SHARJAH

Ordering Information
Quantity sales: Special discounts are available on quantity purchases by corporations, associations, and others. For details, contact the publisher at the address below.

Publisher's Cataloging-in-Publication data
Dust, Adam
The Midnight Mansion

ISBN 9781649797827 (Paperback)
ISBN 9781649797834 (ePub e-book)

Library of Congress Control Number: 2023901575

www.austinmacauley.com/us

First Published 2024
Austin Macauley Publishers LLC
40 Wall Street,33rd Floor, Suite 3302
New York, NY 10005
USA

mail-usa@austinmacauley.com
+1 (646) 5125767

Prologue

Every minute was midnight for the old mansion. There was always a night sky above the weathered roof's shingles. The moon was a constant companion of the structure, its shimmering yellow light cascading through the various outstretched tree limbs. Sometimes outside the mansion, the wind would be cold and sometimes hot. But always the wind would whistle as it navigated its way through the tree branches and scampered across the mansion's ancient red bricks.

There was little light within the mansion. Its princip source was from a seemingly eternal fire that rose and roared from a hearth in the mansion's large reading chamber. Everything in the spacious room – books, tables, chairs, paintings, vases, large floor mirror – maintained a presence secondary to the fireplace. The flames flickered high and low, casting their dancing skill upon the walls and the glass of the solitary window which overlooked the garden in the back of the mansion.

Books were packed, if not jammed, into the large dust-covered bookcase of ancient wood situated in the corner. Some book spines were thick and others thin, while some were red and others blue. Letters of gold and silver highlighted the myriad spines. Volumes included texts about ghosts and magicians. Many ancient alchemists and wizards were gathered on the shelves. The Chronicles of Forbidden Visions by Merchlain was there, holding on its secret pages a plethora of incantations for travels to unholy realms. The book was supposedly cursed and had caused several deaths.

Positioned at the room's far end, a large floor mirror reflected, without opinion, the full contents of the four walls. It watched as the aged green vines of plants climbed walls of peeling faded yellow. The vines only nourishment provided by the window's solar offering on clear days. Occasionally, the silence of the mansion was interrupted by the buzz of a tiny winged intruder that scaled the wall with thin legs before turning to seek an escape from the old place.

The mansion was known to few and had been seen by even fewer. It was spoken of as legend by some in the town of Queensberg and dreamed of by others as nightmares.

Although it could not be proved to be alive, those who spoke of the mansion in trembling whispers were certain it was. The same enigma of life held true for its master.

The mansion was alive with a thousand sounds. The creaking of floorboards for no reason was commonplace. Doors muttered or moaned upon opening. Throughout many yesterdays, doors opened on their own accord at the approach of their master.

The master of the house was a tall, lanky fellow with gaunt, pale features and long blonde hair that draped over his narrow shoulders. He ambled with a limp to his gait and tightly clenched the rail while ascending the stairs. Desperately, he clung to the rail as his weak legs stiffly scaled the steps. His breath was a wheeze that matched every tired step and clicks of his cane. His face's skin was dampened by perspiration. A walk through the mansion was always a long trip. Now it was quite draining and tiring. At least his stomach was now gruesomely filled.

The black coat he wore was tied firmly about his slender hips. It was well worn as it had been used for ages. His gnarled knees knocked together with each step. Finally, he reached the top floor. There he threw open the glass doors to the terrace and breathed in deeply the crisp autumn air. There was an approaching storm on the horizon. Mingling with the scent of recently ripened apples was smoke.

He looked down to see a line of torches wielded by angry townspeople.

Bracing himself against the spiked iron rods of the balcony's rail, he loudly inquired what the strangers wanted. Grease from his recent meal still glistened upon his lips and chin.

"Vengeance…for our children," was the sole shouted reply from a tall bearded man in tattered clothes brandishing a torch before the house was set aflame.

The fire consumed the mansion but did not destroy it or the mystery of the place.

Fast forward to the present minus twenty years.

A small group of teenage children still clad in the Halloween garb from earlier in the evening stood before the scorched remains of the mansion. They discussed their Halloween loot and legends of the cursed scorched husk.

One boy, the youngest of the group, fiddled with the eye patch of his primitive costume as he stared at the imposing remains of the mansion. His pitiful paper hat worn was supposed to say 'pirate' but instead just said 'poor.' He had known true horror brought upon him by several supposed friends.

His imagination made him ignorant of the others until he heard them call to him. He let his eye patch plop back in place and turned to look at the glistening eyes which stared at him.

Beatrice Rham, the eldest of the group, heckled him with taunts of, "Oh, he'll be brave enough to explore the damned place. She had long blonde curls that hung low over sparkling green eyes which could bewitch instantly. She was tall and straight as a board, a condition illuminated by the blue ballerina outfit she wore. Her footwear would make posing on the tips of her toes an ease, but rumors amongst the boys held she was more comfortable as the bottom half of a vertical position."

"Won't you check it out, Chuckie?" Beatrice repeated loudly. She moved to lay a hand on his shoulder, but he rapidly stepped away. He didn't like being touched, especially after what he had endured.

Chuckie nervously surveyed his friends before he finally swallowed hard and agreed to the challenge simply by stating, "I will." Those that watched him either registered a stunned look or laughed as he silently eyed them before defiantly repeating his announcement. Quiet ruled once again as Chuckie's statement had time to resound with all.

Bernie threw the white sheet of ghosthood off his head and stepped forward. "You know you don't have to," he said. "Bea's just being a smart assed bitch. You know how she is."

"I know. But it's okay. I'll do it," Chuckie said and was watched as he walked to the burnt ruins.

Slowly, with a shaking hand, Chuckie reached for the knob of the scorched door. A loud rumbling noise assaulted him and enveloped the kids watching. Carefully, he propped open the rickety door, so as not to let it shut on his small, pink fingers. A bright light escaped the doorway, blurring his form until he disappeared and the light revealed itself as flames. Then his screams echoed throughout the woods, shocking all who stared at the once again newly burnt remains of the old mansion.

Chuckie was never seen again.

Part 1

Reflection 1
Unknown Places and
Yesterday's Mysteries

Bernie breathed heavily. His brown eyes were unfocused as he looked up at the sky blue painted ceiling. There, favored constellations received special treatment in gold paint. His nude body was stretched across the bed with his left leg raised slightly, allowing Tina ample room to apply her tongue tenderly to him. Finally, she raised her head from his crotch. Her apartment was comfortable and welcoming, a nice break from his married life.

Tina licked her lips before giving a quick giggle and laughing aloud, "Yumm, ambrosia of the gods."

He indulged in a quick chuckle with her before rolling over and with one arm embracing her. She repeated her giggle before planting a quick kiss on his lips. His hands firmly flowed down her naked body. His eyes darted along her curves for an erotic inspection which ended with the shockingly sudden ring of his phone.

After giving Tina a quick peck on the cheek, Bernie stood and started for the small wooden nightstand which held the phone. Tina watched him go as she wrapped herself in the aqua blanket. His bare feet pattered across the plush shag rug. In a second, he reached the phone and lifted it to his ear.

He immediately heard the sobbing of his wife Beatrice. For a brief second, he wondered how she had gotten this number.

"What's wrong?" he finally managed to ask after composing himself.

"It's Rickie. He's gone."

"Where…how?" Bernie finally managed to ask in a worried yet composed voice.

"Some of his playmates challenged him to go into the old Charlton mansion and explore the place," Beatrice said between sobs. "He hasn't been seen since."

Bernie inhaled deeply at the mention of the Charlton Mansion. Also known by locals as The Midnight Mansion. It had heralded a multitude of nightmares.

"I'll be there right way," Bernie promised before the line went dead.

***

The heavens seemed to be mourning, if judged by the miniscule beads of snow that assaulted Bernie as he descended the plane's ramp and inhaled the chilly night air of Queensberg. His breath became a haze of cold smoke. In one hand, he grasped a battered old suitcase as he bit his chapped lips. The snow made his hair damp and his heavy trench coat seemed to do little to ward off the chill.

Waiting for him at the airport was his wife. She forced a smile at him before stepping forward to embrace him. She nuzzled her face against his shoulder and used the act to quiet her sobbing. Tears had taken their price on her tired green eyes. Strands of her disheveled hair coated his clothes. He held her in one arm as his other hand loosened its grip on the worn grey suitcase.

The scent about him caused her to say, "Have you been smoking?"

"What do we know," he asked without looking directly into her eyes and ignoring attempted nag.

"Not much," she replied stepping back to allow their eyes to finally form a connection. "However, a driver claimed to see a boy matching his description wandering the old road from the Charlton mansion."

"Damn," Bernie muttered. "Where is the driver now?"

"At the hospital. He's answering police questions and waiting for us," Beatrice replied. "He struck his head against the car's wheel when he veered to avoid the boy and hit a tree. When he looked around, the boy was gone."

"Have you talked to him?" Bernie asked.

His wife nodded.

"Let's go see him and get the hell out of this cold."

***

The cold, quiet was shattered by an ambulance's siren as it sped past the lime green station wagon of Beatrice on the way to the hospital. Beatrice pulled into the hospital's parking lot and stopped her car before yanking the key from the ignition. She threw open her car door. The door echoed in the darkness as it was slammed shut. Bernie climbed out of the car and followed his wife into the hospital.

As they paced down the dimly lit hospital corridors, their footsteps were matched by the squeal of a hospital stretcher's wheels over freshly cleaned floors. The patient on the mobile table ignored all, concerned only with keeping his cover pulled up to their chin. A cleansing scent filled Bernie's nostrils as he recalled previous trips to this place. None of them enjoyable.

Bernie moved to the door of a men's room. Turning to his wife, he muttered, "I just need a moment to compose myself. It seemed a hell of a long flight."

The door swung open with ease. Bernie ignored the wall of mirrors behind the faucets and the single figure standing before them. Above weak lights shone down. He entered the first stall and tried to ignore the banging commotion next to him as well as the female sounding sobs outside.

Bernie finished the need attended to. The next stall commotion quieted but the crying remained. Bernie exited the stall and slowly approached the solitary, slender figure by the row of faucets. He believed it was a woman due to her long red-hued hair and the long scarlet fingernails which covered her face.

"Are you all right, miss?" he tentatively inquired before adding, "This is the men's room. I think you must have entered the wrong room."

She became quiet and turned to him. Just then, he noticed for the first time that she cast no reflection in the mirror. Removing her hands from her , he saw blue eyes, a small nose, and rich red lips that trembled. All was captured on a pale canvas. He guessed her to be in her early twenties.

Her hands lowered to her sides as she announced, "The end is not near. The end is here."

She finished her statement with a scream as her red nails reached for him. She threw her head back and opened her mouth to reveal fangs that glistened in the light.

Bernie moved back and turned toward the door of the stall, he had heard the noise from opened to reveal the bloody body of a bald man in a brown suit crawl desperately forth. Like a macabre slug, the man left a path of blood behind.

A scream caught in Bernie's throat as he barreled out the door to find Beatrice in a quiet hospital hall.

"Are you okay?" Beatrice inquired as Bernie ran a hand over his flushed face.

"After what I've been through? I think so."

"What have you been through?"

"A man was bleeding badly and a woman…"

"A woman? But that's the men's room."

"I don't think she was really a woman. She was a vampire, only interested in my blood."

"Well from your smell, I suspect you were smoking," Beatrice said as she moved closer and sniffed. "And from this delusion, I suspect you were drinking."

"Then take a look," Berne demanded as he threw open the men's room door to reveal it as clean and empty.

"I think we should get moving and you should keep quiet," Beatrice said before striding off.

Bernie again opened the men's room door and took a second to look around only to find nothing.

Obediently, Bernie followed his wife to a tall and youthful police officer at the door to the room of the stranger who thought he may have seen Rickie. The officer's only motion was a nod to them as they entered.

Within a brown bearded man wearing a hospital gown sat up in bed, talking excitedly despite the tired look on his broad face. In a chair to his right was seated a man clad in a well-tailored brown suit who wore round spectacles which highlighted his pale face's chiseled features. He had long blond hair with greying tips. A cane with a derby handle was propped against his chair. At the couple's approach, he shifted his seated position and turned his attention from the patient to them.

"Hello," said the seated stranger before pulling a card from his pocket and offering it to Bernie. Bernie looked at the card which simply read Dr. Solomon Carlton – psychiatrist. "I've been requested to aid with the investigation."

"Thank you," mumbled Bernie as he removed his wallet from his coat and placed the card inside before removing a picture of little Rickie which he held up toward the bedridden man. "Is this the boy you saw?"

The patient sat up further to get a better look before nodding. "I was just returning from a party and only glanced at the lad for a second, but I think that's him."

"He already identified him from a picture his mother brought," Carlton quietly commented.

***

The guard at the doorway came to an alert stance as the married couple exited the hospital room.

"We're just going to the cafeteria," Bernie explained, exhausted looks on both his and his wife's faces.

"Anything learned?" the police officer asked.

"Not really," replied Bernie with a tired shake of his head.

"Too bad," the officer commented as he reached for his hand radio. "I suppose I should contact the captain. He wants to stay in touch with details of the case."

A nurse approached the door and asked, "Is the patient sleeping?"

"No," Bernie answered. "He's talking with the psychiatrist."

Both officer and nurse offered a stunned look.

"Who?" the officer asked.

"The psychiatrist," Bernie repeated.

"There has been no psychiatrist here," the officer replied before pushing past Bernie into a room empty save for a motionless patient lying on the bed.

"But the psychiatrist was here. We both talked to him," Bernie muttered in explanation as he and his wife followed the officer and confusedly glanced about the quiet room.

The nurse's eyes settled on the still patient. Slowly, she moved forward and grasped the cold wrist.

"He said his name was Carlton. He gave me his card," Bernie explained to the officer as he withdrew his wallet. Opening it, he produced a card that was blank on both sides. "This was it. It had his name and occupation on it. I know it."

Frazzled, Bernie ran a hand through his dark hair until a voice broke the silence.

"He's dead," the nurse proclaimed as she stepped away from the bed.

Part 2

Rickie awoke amid numerous blankets of finely stitched details on a large bed in a room of scarlet painted walls. The room was dark, save for a stream of silver moonlight that trailed in through a narrow window opposite the four-poster beds. Looking about, Rickie found the red-painted room to be desolate save for empty dressers gnarled of antique appearance and several small side tables of ancient wood. The walls were decorated with large oil paintings depicting lavish forest scenes and nude women.

Holding his breath for unknown reasons, Rickie slowly moved off the bed and found his way to the heavy door of wood. Its old brass knob wouldn't turn easily, but with both hands and some force, Rickie managed to shove it open. He slowly stuck his head out into the hallway. It was slender and featured copious cobwebs illuminated by torches adorning the walls which also featured old oil paintings highlighting nature.

A cool breeze drifted down the hallway as Rickie slowly paced down the dust-ridden corridor. A bump beneath the thick black carpet resulted in a trip but not a fall. Each step was muffled by the thick midnight-colored carpet. His footprints left their imprints in the carpet, showing his slow path to a door beneath which a bright light trickled forth.

Nervously, Rickie placed his hand on the cold doorknob. He gave it a quick turn. The door easily opened.

Within the door, there was a large wooden table. It was covered with a white table cloth. Golden goblets and dishes sat upon it. The bigger dishes held thickly carved meats and large pieces of fruits. Rickie pulled out a finely carved chair with a red cushion and sat.

Seated at the table was a lad with long brown hair and the shaggy stubble of an immature beard. He was dressed in a tattered and torn pirate costume with a cheap paper hat angled atop his head while an old patch dangled below one eye. He poked his tarnished and bent fork into the gruel on his plate which he ravenously devoured via loud gulps. The dirty costume was at least a size too small as it failed to reach his thin wrists while barely confining his hefty stomach.

As he dipped a large spoon into the bowel of gruel sitting in the middle of the table, he turned to Rickie, as if noticing him for the first time and asked, "Do you want some?"

Rickie shook his head while his tight lips remained silent. The shaggily stubbled youth simply shrugged his shoulder in response and shoveled more gruel onto his golden plate.

Rickie leaned forward in his chair and looked into the swirling red liquid placed in the goblet by the plate that sat in front of him. He picked up the goblet and raised it to his nose. A sniff proved the scent unenticing. Slowly raising the goblet to his lips, he took a quick sip. The taste was no more appealing than the scent. Quickly, he returned the goblet to its place, followed by several loud coughs.

Then the only sound which intruded on the quiet room was the enthusiastic chewing by the boy in the sad pirate outfit until a door at the opposite end of where Rickie sat opened with a loud squeak.

The heavy sound of shuffling footfalls was matched by the sound of a cane striking the stone floor.

The new arrival had long blond hair and wore spectacles. He was clad in a well-tailored brown suit over which flowed a heavily worn black coat.

"Hungry, Chuckie?" the new arrival inquired with a sinister smile.

Chuckie grunted with a nod that didn't slow his intake of gruel.

"And what of you?" the man with the cane added as he looked at Rickie.

"I'm not hungry," Rickie replied before pushing himself away from the table. None at it bothered with a look at him. "I just want to go home."

"Just think of this as your second home. Chuckie does as he's been here and happy for so long. How long has it been?"

"I don't remember, Dr. Charlton," Chuckie said as he dropped some gruel on his sleeve without bothering to notice it.

"There, you see he doesn't even remember," Dr. Charlton said with a laugh.

Chuckie looked up at Charlton and began to laugh as well.

Soon only Rickie failed to join in the laughter.

Charlton collapsed into a cushioned seat at the end of the table, his head swiveling about to take in the full view of his guests. The chair squeaked as he adjusted his weight in it.

"Who wants to play a game?" he asked.

A clang echoed as Chuckie dropped his old fork. "Hide and seek?" Chuckie loudly asked.

Charlton nodded as his lips twisted to a sinister smile.

"I will," Chuckie said as a wicked grin spread over his lips.

Charlton leaned forward. "That means you, Rickie are IT. You've got to hide. You'll find plenty of spots in the mansion," Charlton explained with a sly smile that was part of a wicked expression. "Go."

Rickie stood up and backed away from the table.

"Run!" Chuckie roared in demand as he pushed his bowl away and banged a fist against the table.

Startled and frightened, Rickie turned. He dashed out of the door he had entered.

Chuckie watched before approaching Carlton and laying his head in the doctor's lap. Charlton muttered, "We'll give him a few minutes, and then you can begin your pursuit. I'm sure you'll get him…like the others."

Part 3

As Chuckie relaxed in Charlton's lap, he remembered as if it were a long-ago dream how he first encountered Dr. Charlton in a time before he eternally resided in the midnight mansion.

Weeds and other small plants were trampled by small sneakered feet as the children pursued Chuckie through the dim light of the branch-covered forest. Small squirrels and turtles watched from beneath damp crevices covered in part by leaves of myriad colors. Birds fluttered through tree limbs but gave no song for unfolding events below.

The children clutched broken branches and flung rocks at their quarry. Chuckie moaned aloud to himself as one stone struck the back of his head. There was already a bruise on his face and multiple marks beneath his small, soiled shirt. His legs were red from scratches accumulated in the mad flight through the foliage frenzy which occurred in the woods.

A tall boy with reddish hair led the boys to chase Chuckie. He wore a button-down orange short sleeve shirt and blue shorts. He was a ferocious fighter and mean leader called Marty. Marty's teeth were sharp and a dark yellow. His ears appeared pointed giving him a vicious elf look.

Eventually, the fastest of his pursuers caught up with Chuckie whose fat, legs buckled as the weight of the other boy brought him down. Chuckie lay struggling on the cold earth and the others boys soon surrounded him. Blows from clenched fists pummeled Chuckie as he was helplessly twisted. Marty grinned. It was Chuckie's wish to break free…to strike Marty and possibly make that grin a bit less frightening by one tooth.

"Hold him down," Marty instructed.

The gang followed instructions with harsh laughter as Chuckie felt hands clench his arms and legs.

"Want a smoke?" Marty asked as his grimy hands fished a packet of cigarettes out of a dirty pocket. Without fumbling, he opened the packet and withdrew several cigarettes. He produced several matches and efficiently lit one. "Or just fire?"

Chuckie's eyes grew large with horror as his shorts grew wet.

Finally, as Chuckie's struggling slowed a bit, Marty barked instructions to his wicked compatriots. "He's ready for play. Let's finish him up. You know what to do."

Chuckie closed his eyes. He heard his clothes rip. His flesh grew cold.

His bare bottom was hoisted up.

He felt blows and pinches upon his bare skin.

It couldn't be too bad. After all, girls took it all the time. One day he'd have a girl.

Then all became quiet.

A gentle wind caressed his bare body. Finally, he opened his eyes.

He was alone in the woods save for a tall man with long blond hair who clutched a cane.

"Are you okay?" the man asked.

Chuckie pushed himself upward with his elbows and nodded.

"Good," the man said as he stared at Chuckie with dark eyes that were somehow forbidding. Chuckie sensed he'd get to know those eyes well. Perhaps too well.

"My name is Dr. Charlton," the stranger said as he offered his hand to the bewildered boy.

Chuckie took it. Slowly he stood. Both ignored his nakedness.

"Come with me."

Then he felt Charlton's hand move beneath his chin.

The clap of the doctor's hands signaled that the time to rest and remember was done. The search was to begin.

***

The cold blade of the razor pressed against the bare skin of his jaw. Bernie ignored the brisk sensation as he watched himself in the bathroom mirror. Eyes were almost as bright as usual, surprisingly considering the past few days. Hairline only slightly receding but still thick. The razor rapidly broke the surface of the water in the sink basin.

With a swirl, the sharp instrument mixed into the shaving cream-covered water which also contained short brown strands of hair and a slight bit of blood. Bernie exhaled deeply as he looked at himself in the mirror. Completely clean-shaven now plus a somewhat firm and flat upper torso. He took a towel from a rack and wiped his face.

Behind him stood Beatrice, silently watching. He hung the towel back on the rack and turned to her. "You okay?" he asked.

"Not so good," she replied.

"Sorry," he answered without looking directly at her. "The bathroom's all yours now."

"You could have joined me last night," she said. "Our bedroom is just as you left it."

"I was all right in the guest room. I've gotten used to it," he said with a meager smile.

"Still good with the divorce?" she asked.

"I think it's what's best for us," he answered with a nod.

"What happened to us?" she wondered aloud.

His only answer was a tired roll of his head.

"I keep thinking of the past."

"Ours?" he asked.

"Yes," she said. "And of other things."

He reached for her arms draped in a blue robe she wore and grasped her.

"Rickie's all right," he assured her without loosening his grip. "I'm sure the town's curse hasn't touched him. I hate this damned place."

"I guess that's why you wanted to get away so badly. It wasn't just me."

"No," Bernie muttered as he placed a kiss on her cheek.

Beatrice smiled as her hands massaged his back.

***

As Rickie ran through the cobweb cloaked corridors of the dark old house, his small hands gently patted against the dust-strewn walls. His breath came in heavy gasps which could not quite be seen in the ancient house's poor light and frigid atmosphere.

Chuckie puffed as he ungainly scampered along after his prey. Heavy legs pumped desperately forward at an awkward pace. A horrid grin distorted his face as he finally glimpsed Rickie ahead.

Upon nearing Rickie, he lurched forward. The collision brought the two boys down. Rickie grumbled as he struggled, finally flipping over beneath his opponent who he grasped beneath the jaw to push away.

Chuckie made a sinister smile which Rickie stared at from below. Chuckie released the struggling youngster and sat back. Chuckie crossed his arms. For a second, he relaxed on his haunches.

Suddenly, there was a cigarette in Chuckie's grimy hand. The boy then produced a lighter. He smiled as the instrument ignited, spewing forth a flame into the darkness.

The fire touched the cigarette before Chuckie returned the lighter to a torn, dirty pocket. A knife, whose blade shined in the firelight, was now in Chuckie's hand. Rickie struggled until he shivered from the cold either provided by the house's low temperature or the knife against his neck.

But the knife did not remain still.

In a second, it cleaved Rickie's left ear free.

Rickie screamed as he clenched his bloody head but he could not roll free from Chuckie.

Part 4

The car ground to a stop atop the gravel, launching small stones in all directions. A deer cocked his head toward the vehicle before abandoning interest and scampering off. Bernie stepped out of the car with a crunching sound made by his foot upon the loose rocks that formed the primitive drive.

Bernie's breath came in cloudy puffs as he surveyed the desolate scene. A touch of snow mingled with frost to cover the ground. Trees with bare limbs stood at attention about the area and a large white house solitarily adorned the lonely ridge.

Beatrice noted the lonely house as she stepped out of the car and slammed the door. The noise brought Bernie's attention back to reality and the car. Scattered in the back seat were several toys and books aimed at young readers.

Bernie buttoned the top of his jacket and turned to Beatrice. He clasped his hands together and rubbed for warmth. "Are you sure this is a good idea?" he asked. "What do you know about her?"

"She's a well-respected historian and was quite helpful when I met with her about the history of the Charlton house a few days ago. The town's curse has touched her, too. Her child recently disappeared," Beatrice said as she turned to

Bernie. "She also has the gift of second sight which she has shared with me."

Bernie shrugged and waved his hands in acceptance. Beatrice was most familiar with the motion.

The two left the car in the drive and started up the walkway of chipped stone to the wooden front door. Once there, Beatrice stepped aside for Bernie to knock. Bernie turned to his wife as he tried to listen for sounds from within.

"Are you sure the meeting was set for here and now?" he asked.

She replied with a decisive nod but did not remove her eyes from the door.

Finally, the sound of heavy footsteps was heard from within followed by the sound of locks being released. The door creaked open to reveal a short, stout lady with a white streak in her hair. A pair of round gold wired glasses rested on her small nose and a rich red lipstick colored her mouth. Smiling, she said, "Welcome. Come in out of the cold."

She stepped back and held the door open for them. Bernie was first in and glanced about at the warmly painted pink walls and comfortably aged furniture. Oddly, an empty birdcage hung from a pole at one corner. The only clue of a child's presence was the presence of copious stuffed animals strewn throughout the room.

"My name is Rachel Milburn. I'm the town librarian. Also I assume I'm the town historian if needed," she said in her squeakily pleasant voice. "I'm so sorry about your boy."

"Thank you," Beatrice replied as she took the historian's hand.

Rachel brushed back the beads hanging from the opposite doorway and led them into a dark room. The walls were painted with dreary grey. Heavy curtains decorated each window, blocking the view of the outside world. In the center of the room was a small round table of wood. The table's smooth surface shined. Atop it sat a crystal ball in a metal stand. Tarot cards were scattered at the base of the stand. Rachel pulled out a chair. She sat down, spreading her arms to indicate the others join her. Beatrice rapidly did.

With a tired sigh, Bernie added his tired presence. Only one chair was now left empty.

Beatrice leaned toward Rachel and whispered, "Tell him the story of the house as you told me."

Rachel nodded. Then leaned forward, baby blue eyes focusing on Bernie. "According to town records, the house was built around 1800 by a doctor Solomon Charlton."

"I'm familiar with that name," Bernie said leaning forward with hands flat on the table. Beatrice's stare remained on Rachel.

"Well, this guy was no respectable doctor. Reports questioned whether he was any kind of doctor or just a quack. He supposedly had a slew of elixirs and tonics to treat any conceivable condition. Plus he dabbled in alchemy and sorcery. He perfected a way through these means to have time stand still for the house. It was said that no matter what time one entered the house, one could look outside and find it a night. Even astronomical signs remained in a fixed state."

"Quite the magician," Bernie grumbled with a roll of his eyes.

"He was almost a 100 when he moved here, according to legend. Practically immortal. And evil. It seemed he had a taste for children."

"How so?" Bernie asked nervously.

"He lured the town's children into the house never to be seen again. Some rumors were that he sexually abused them. Other stories said he ate them."

Beatrice let out a pained screech as she fell forward onto the table. As she sobbed madly, Bernie seized her shoulders and massaged them while suggesting she take deep breaths.

"Finally, the townspeople couldn't take it anymore. A mob confronted Carlton. They burned the house down. But it is rumored that Charlton lived on."

"A possible cannibal for good measure who still spreads his bitter brand of love around here. But what of our son? Can you help us find him? Where should we look?"

"The remains of Charlton's burnt house is where you should look. It is his point of nexus with this realm. But as he has a connection with midnight at the house, that is when you should search. Of course, it might already be too late."

Bernie shoved himself away from the table glancing at his still sobbing wife and adding, "Let' get out of here."

She failed to move as he stood. Finally, she looked up at him as he headed toward the door and held out an open hand to her. She rose meekly, as did Rachel.

"You realize you can't just run away from this," Rachel said as she followed them. "He can be everywhere."

Beatrice embraced her husband, then turned back to Rachel. "I do want to thank you for all your help. All the information you've provided," Beatrice softly said, her eyes were still downcast as if seeking a mound to hide behind.

Rachel patted Beatrice encouragingly on the shoulder before producing a Kleenex. Beatrice breathed in heavily and looked up with a forced smile before taking the Kleenex with which to wipe her moist nose and eyes. "Thank you."

"Let me know if you ever need me," Rachel said. "For information or anything," Rachel added with a smile. "Remember, the supernatural and magic exists."

"Thank you," Beatrice repeated.

Both Beatrice and her husband nodded at Rachel before leaving. The door closed, cutting off a gust of cold wind. Rachel turned and with a sigh approached the couch from which she picked up a miniature red fox toy. A tear formed in her eye as she clutched the stuffed animal and dealt with a flood of memories.

Then there was a knock at the door. She let the fox drop to the couch and stepped away. She expected to see Beatrice and Bernie standing in the doorway but, instead, there was a young boy clad in a tattered pirate Halloween costume who toyed with a knife. His head only reached her waist, his battered paper pirate hat a bit higher. The blade glittered brightly in the old porch light. The light revealed a wicked grin on the child's face as with one hand, he apparently juggled the knife.

"Hello?" she quizzically inquired.

The boy said nothing as his wicked smile grew.

"You know today isn't Halloween," she said sweetly with a touch of sarcasm.

The boy made a fine gesture of letting the knife plop back firmly onto his hand. He lunged forward and slashed at her once with his sharp, shiny blade, but struck only empty air. Rachel gasped as she stepped back in astonishment.

Then, still clutching his knife by its beautiful hilt, he turned and scampered off the porch.

Rachel confusedly looked around but saw nothing save darkness as she listened to the quiet. Then she tightly shut the door and twisted a few locks on it. She tiredly braced her back against the door and sighed. She ran a hand over her face. There was no nervous perspiration, but she was sure there soon would be.

The stillness of the house was interrupted by a bang from behind her that shook the door and brought her to attention. She spun around as a new knock sounded at the door.

Slowly she reached for the doorknob. She twisted it without breathing.

The door opened to reveal a finely dressed man of gaunt, pale features clutching a walking stick. The wind rustled his long, white-tipped hair. Rachel glanced about but could see no second figure.

"Yes?" Rachel inquired.

"I thought it was time we finally met," he said.

"I want my daughter," Rachel demanded without moving, a stern look painting her face.

"One day," he mused with an unfriendly smile that seemed to have more in common with a wolf leading its pack on a hunt than a person.

Part 5

Bernie awoke without feeling refreshed. The guest room looked the same as when he had departed a year ago. The faded Victorian pictures were the same. The peeling peach paint was the same. The creaking old bed and the old green quilt were the same. The only difference was that he was now using them.

Bernie rose and pulled back the curtains next to the bed to reveal the small fountain and apple trees. The sun's light filtered through the cloudy sky and glass to his bare chest. The warmth was minor but felt good. He stepped away from the window. The little blue phone on the night stand rang.

"Yes," Bernie softly said into the receiver.

"How is it going?" Tina asked in her high and jovial voice. A second of silence followed. Then she added, "Do you want me to join you?"

"No, it's okay."

"Are you sure? I can catch a plane today."

"No," he rapidly replied. "Everything's fine."

"What have you found out about Rickie?"

"Not much," he rapidly retorted in a tired voice. "I'll call you tomorrow."

"All right," she said followed by the smacking sound of lips and then the empty nothing of a deadline.

Bernie returned the receiver to the phone and looked up to see Beatrice. No surprise or anger marked her face.

"How did she get this number?" Beatrice asked.

"She has it for emergencies," Bernie answered. "I would suppose this business with Rickie qualifies."

"I would agree."

"How long have you known about her?"

"Since the beginning of the affair. You were away all too often at your agents. And Rachel saw details of what was happening."

Turning away, Bernie grabbed his shirt and walked away announcing, "I need a drink."

"Isn't it a little early to start?" Beatrice coldly asked as she motionlessly watched him dress.

"I'm just going to have an orange juice," he replied. "Although I recall your happy hour started swiftly after dawn." Bernie departed.

Beatrice wandered into the kitchen. There, Bernie clenched his glass of orange juice in both hands.

Bernie looked up and asked, "Can I get you something? Jack Daniels or has your tastes changed?"

"I've been sober for years. It was easier when you left."

"Ah, flaming arrow at one o'clock," Bernie commented before a large gulp of juice as Beatrice strode toward him.

"I'm going to go check out the scorched house remains as Rachel suggested. Are you coming or would you rather lounge here with your juice and wait for another call from your gal?"

Bernie swallowed the last of the juice from his glass and slammed the glass to the table. "Let's go," he said as he rose. He stepped toward his wife, placing his hands on her hips and leaning forward for a kiss.

"Are you feeling horny or just checking my breath for alcohol?" she asked bitterly.

Bernie stepped back from her. "Let's go."

The car came to a halt on the dirt road next to the house's scorched remains. Bernie and Beatrice stepped out of the car. The breeze chilled as it swirled through the trees. The bright sun above provided little warmth as the married couple trudged through brown grass both thick and high.

They took turns calling out their son's name. With sunglasses or hands, they shielded their eyes as they scanned the woods. The forest housed many dark spots of shadows, to maintain its secrets. Occasionally, they received their own shout returned to them in an echo, but that was the most return they got.

"Where is he," Bernie growled to himself as with frustrated disdain he kicked an old beer bottle in the almost overgrown path. The sound of the old bottle rolling over rocks reverberated in the quiet of the mysterious woods.

Beatrice turned to her husband and commented, "My opinion of the stuff now too."

"Indeed."

"A pity we don't have any of your new party favorites. But needles can be hard to come by."

"That was the past. I was experimenting. Can you blame me? The life of a commercial jingle writer isn't all caviar on sunny seaside beaches."

Beatrice nodded. She was silent a moment as her eyes scanned the horizon. Then she added, "How is your new experiment going?"

"New one?" he asked as he turned back toward her.

"Tina?"

Both pairs of eyes returned to the surroundings as they continued their search in silence.

***

Beatrice closed her eyes in the enjoyment of the silence disrupted solely by the sound of the shower's water as it fell. The water struck the slick tub floor and her nude body.

The moments were lonely ones. But time continued and she decided she did not need the shower.

With a decisive and quick twist of the wrist, she brought the shower to an abrupt end. Beatrice stepped from the tub, her wet feet marking the matt. She slipped her feet into a pair of fuzzy slippers. It had been quite a while since those feet had been in ballerina shoes. Or even any kind of dancing shoes.

She glanced at the scales. Instead of approaching the tiny metallic beast, she sighed while pulling her fluffiest towel from the wrack. She patted her curved body dry. In her youth and first years of marriage, it had been thinner. She buried her face in the towel. Between her husband's recent behavior and the mystery of her child's disappearance, she felt like hiding. Instead, she dried her locks of hair.

Beatrice patted her body dry. Finally allowing the towel to drop, she reached for her aqua robe and slipped it on. She left the warm bathroom and descended the stairs to the cool living room. There Bernie sat in a recliner with an open magazine propped up in his lap.

"Feel better?" he quietly asked.

"Not with all that's going on."

Reaching the bottom of the steps, she crossed the room and opened a mini-refrigerator by the bar. She grabbed a glass from the bar and filled it with orange juice. "Want something to drink?"

Bernie shook his head. Without interest, he looked down at the magazine. At last, he turned the page.

"Where could he be?" she asked herself aloud. "We looked everywhere in that forest today."

"We can search again tomorrow. Maybe we should call your friend for advice. I'm sure Rachel would love to help," he said mockingly.

Beatrice looked at him with fierce eyes. "I'm sure she'd be more help than you."

Bernie nodded and tossed the magazine away to an end table before laying his head on the back of the chair.

A loud knock at the door disrupted the house's silence. Both Beatrice and Bernie looked up, but neither made another reaction until the second knock.

Beatrice drained the last of her drink and abandoned her glass on the bar as she announced, "I'll get it."

Opening the door revealed two police officers. One was tall with a dark mustache. The other was bald and portly.

"Mrs. Pierpont?" the mustached officer asked.

"Yes," Beatrice promptly replied.

"We have a few questions for you."

"Oh, about my son's disappearance," Beatrice said as she stepped back, allowing the door to open further. "We've been searching the woods for him all day with no luck, I'm afraid."

"Son?" the mustached officer said with some confusion.

Beatrice nodded. She sadly attempted to hide her befuddlement.

"I'm sorry to disturb you at this time but we're here about a murder," the officer said.

"A murder?" Beatrice muttered as Bernie rose to his feet, interest piqued.

"Is this your husband?" the officer asked while Bernie stepped forward.

"Yes," Beatrice softly replied with a nod as Bernie approached the doorway.

"We need to speak with you both at the station. I'm afraid both of your fingerprints were found at the crime scene," the mustached officer explained.

"What crime scene?" Bernie asked as his face twisted with confusion. "Who was murdered?"

"A local lady named Rachel Milburn. She was tied up and practically butchered by knife wounds."

Part 6

The coroner breathed heavily as he circled the dimly lit metal table which displayed Rachel Milburn's bloody corpse. He repeatedly pushed the steel-rimmed glasses higher on his thin, pointed nose. It was about time for a new pair.

He uncovered a plate beside the table which revealed several sparkling instruments. One was a small knife with a slender blade. The coroner picked it up. He sighed, noting the body was covered by bloody wounds.

The sound of footsteps along with a clip-clop clatter from the hall behind him caught his attention. He turned, gripping the knife tighter.

The door slammed open revealing a long-haired older man in a suit. With one hand, he gripped a cane that clicked upon the polished grey floor as he approached the autopsy table.

"Who the hell are you?" the coroner asked in a wavering voice.

With a quick movement, his cane struck the coroner's hand and triggered the flight of the knife.

The stranger bent over the autopsy table and eyed well the mutilated body. "Accidents must happen," he muttered quietly to himself before finally taking his eyes off the body and looking up.

"My name is Charlton. Nice to meet you, sir," he said as he straightened up.

"You shouldn't be here. Get the fuck out."

Suddenly, the force of a mysterious breeze slammed the door open and Chuckie appeared still dressed in the tattered remains of the pirate costume from the long-ago Halloween. In his hand, he held a knife. It was bloody.

"This is my boy, Chuckie," Charlton said, his arm outstretched.

"Stand back," stuttered the coroner, still massaging his struck hand. He moved back but was stopped by the table.

"Oh, it's all right," Carlton commented as he smiled at Chuckie. "The boy has a fondness for macabre things."

Chuckie revealed his teeth with a grin as he jumped forward, slashing his blade back and forth in the coroner's direction.

Carlton continued an examination of Milburn's body, ignoring Chuckie's macabre actions or the coroner's screams.

***

Although only two floors above, the interrogation room that housed Bernie with two officers was quiet. One officer, a gangly pimple marked blond, leaned back and stretched his arms. His yarn rivaled the chair's creak to break the silence of the room until his partner spoke.

"When was the last time you saw your son?"

"The holiday season, last year," Bernie tiredly replied.

"Everything went okay?"

"I guess. He seemed happy enough."

The bald questioning officer leaned forward and asked, "But you don't see him often?"

"No. His mother and I are separated."

The other officer asked, "Are you getting divorced?"

Bernie rolled his eyes and nodded.

"Have you begun…another relationship?"

"What the hell does that have to do with anything?" Bernie angrily asked as he rose to his feet.

"Probably nothing, we're just trying to get all the facts," the officer replied before offering a calming smile. "Did you know Milburn?"

Bernie shook his head.

"Did you have any experience with her special abilities? She was supposedly a psychic."

"She was a kook," the other officer inserted.

"I met her once but never knew her," Bernie said.

"How was she when you met her? Did you see anyone else there?"

"No. It was a brief meeting. She seemed fine to me. My wife had consulted her about our son's disappearance."

"Anything else?"

"I suppose she was also interested in learning more about our personal business."

"I bet," added the other officer as he let out a gruff guffaw.

"Do you know who your son was with when he was last seen?"

"Some fellow kids he was trick-or-treating with. Then a motorist supposedly saw him in the road."

"The driver in question is dead. Did you know him?"

"No," Bernie exclaimed before jumping to his feet. He knocked the chair back. "We searched the woods for Rickie all yesterday, but it was no use. I just want to get out there and look for him again if you can't find him."

"Sit down and calm yourself," an officer suggested.

"Am I free?" Bernie asked, pacing bout the interrogation room.

"Your wife has just been released and now you may join her." Both officers rose to look Bernie in the eyes. "We'll continue the investigation. Just remember, neither of you is to leave town."

***

Rickie awoke enveloped in darkness and pain. The cold stuck daggers in his chest with every breath. The sound was muffled by the gauze tied around his head. It was stained by blood from his severed ear.

He found movement difficult, due to the chains that tied his arms.

With heavy pants, he managed to push himself to his feet so that he stood in the emptiness. He heard the soft squeak of a mouse at his foot before he felt it scamper over his barefoot. A scream bubbled up in his throat to escape for no one to hear.

Desperately, he glanced about for his mother.

For his father.

Again, he helplessly screamed at the emptiness.

***

Beatrice stood at the police station's front window watching the rainfall. She put her hand against the glass pane water splattered against, feeling cold but nothing else.

The sound behind her caused her to turn. Bernie emerged from a hall, tired with disappointment etched on his face. As he approached her, he said only, "I'm out of here."

"They said they'd give us a drive back…" Beatrice began.

"I'll take a cab," Bernie said as he spun around. "I want to be alone."

"You are coming home?" she mildly asked.

"Is there a home to go to?"

Putting her arms around his neck, she replied, "Of course there is."

"Okay then," he unbelievingly relented with a sigh. "See you there. I'll call a cab."

***

With the cold rain and sleet slashing away, catching a cab wasn't the easiest objective, but Bernie accomplished it before being soaked. He ran a hand through his damp hair and breathed heavily while watching the city's lights blur past. The lights merged with water streaks to create an odd urban landscape.

Bernie enjoyed the quiet. To think unrushed was divine.

However, the fair sex intruded in his mind's eye. He saw Tina clad in white panties and posed provocatively on a large bed. Her skin was smooth and white, always enticingly warm to the touch. Bernie closed his eyes remembering the beauty revealed when the panties were removed. All would then be erotically enticing as he was beckoned forth onto her. His reverie was harshly interrupted by the cabbie's announcement of charge as the car pulled to a halt.

Bernie fished out the money from his wallet and handed it to the driver saying, "Keep the change."

Turning to take the cash, the driver grinned. As Bernie buttoned his jacket's collar, the driver said, "Thanks loads, bud."

Bernie stepped out of the car into the frantic weather. He noted that the house's windows revealed no lights. Bernie stared at the cab when he heard its wheels squeal off. Then his attention returned to the house. Bernie took a deep breath before approaching it. His shoes squeaked on the wet sidewalk. The steps of the front porch seemed higher than his last ascent of them.

He slid his key into the doorknob and twisted it. The door opened easily but he still missed the doors of the hotels he stayed at where an electronic key card was just placed against the lock. The door opened as easy as if an ancient mage pronounced the magic words, "open me."

Bernie found himself in darkness and still recalled the easy route through the house. No radar was needed. As Bernie approached the door of the guest room, he found the darkness intensified as he felt something warm against his head.

"Welcome back," he heard Beatrice say as she covered his eyes. She switched the light on. In seconds Bernie adjusted to the light.

Before him, he saw his wife's nude form. She stood still with arms now folded behind her bare body. Bernie's left eyebrow raised as his eyes traveled over her form. Not as thin as she appeared when they first married but still fit.

Bernie stepped forward and dropped to his knees.

She smiled as her eyes followed him. Her smile grew as her head fell back and her hand found the head whose mouth ravished her between the legs. He devoured her intimate flavors and scents before rising. He lifted her off her feet and lumbered through darkness to the bed.

Part 7

Water dripped from the stalactites. A splatter was made either as it hit the hard stone or pools accumulated below. Blood from wounds mixed with water.

Weak and bewildered, Rickie found movement difficult due to the metal chains fastened to his wrists. His head ached as his wound felt as though it were on fire. Where his left ear once was, only a quagmire of blood and scabs remained.

After a moment of staring into the darkness, he believed he could see something.

The brief bright glint aided in focusing on the subject.

Chuckie stood before him with the knife in hand. "Wanna play," he growled gruffly.

Rickie's head dropped tiredly back to lay in the blood and water gathered on the stone below. Then he leaped up. His old ripped sneakers slipped as he attempted to race away. Rickie felt a small yet firm hand grasp his left leg. The lad lurched forward till his head met the cold, hard stone.

His knee painfully throbbed as blood crept down his torn pant leg.

Seeing was useless but he heard more rips off his clothing.

His legs were helpless as a sharp pain ignited in his right side.

***

Bernie and Beatrice were exhausted from fighting for every footstep through the overgrown foliage of the forest when despite twilight a startling sight met their exhausted eyes. Before them, a large fashionable-looking mansion replaced burnt remains.

"Do you see what I think I see?" Bernie quietly asked. Beatrice nodded.

She brushed back some overhanging leaves of an adjacent tree and stepped forward. As she approached the immaculately restored mansion, a light flicked on in a window.

"Do you see that?" she asked.

Before Bernie could answer, a large green serpent with massive front fangs dropped out of the overhanging tree. Bernie clutched its muscular body even as it entwined him, its loop about his neck tightened.

Beatrice stepped onto the front porch as she placed her hand on the door's knob. The barrier opened with a creak.

For a second, Beatrice stared into what was now darkness. But beyond old furniture and a shadowy reflection offered by a large, circular mirror, she could see nothing.

"I get an eerie feeling. Now it is night with the moon overhead. Something strange is going on here," she said. Turning, she saw Bernie gasping for breath as he writhed on the ground against the serpent. The creature's flickering tongue moistened his cheek. "Bernie!"

Beatrice raced off the porch toward Bernie. Her knees landed in the dirt as she grasped the serpent beneath its head. As it loosened, it held on Bernie, she pulled it away. With a sigh of exhaustion, she heaved it into the high grass of the woods.

The creature laid stunned on the ground a moment, then curled its body up. Re-orientated, it slowly crawled off.

Bernie sat up and gasped at his wife as she knelt by him. Her hand wiped the dirt from his face and then played with his hair. He put his arms around her. Deeply, he inhaled her familiar scent and smiled.

Feeling a sudden intense desire, he pulled her close. Close enough for each to experience the sensation of the other's pounding heart. But that was not all Beatrice felt. She fell back onto the ground beneath her husband and felt his cool hand reach beneath her clothing.

She sighed, happily anticipating his hands' fondling. Her breath came in quicker pants. His touch became more demanding.

Finally, her chest was exposed to him as her hips grinded against him. His hands became moist with perspiration.

Her head moved upward toward him as he slipped her pants down. Her lips opened slightly but she made no sound. The speech was unimportant as their lips found other uses.

He repeated his action as on the ground, in her arms as touching her felt comfortable. Good. Safe.

He became immune to all other sounds or actions until she abruptly sat up. The pale moon reflected in her eyes as she pointed nervously at the light that now eerily shone through spider webs on one of the mansion's windows.

Bernie reluctantly pulled himself off her and stared at the light.

"I may hate myself for this," he muttered aloud as he turned to Beatrice while adjusting his clothes, "But let's check it out."

Beatrice nodded and followed her husband into the mansion as an owl let out a hoot while perched high in the gnarled branches of an ancient tree.

By the time Bernie and Beatrice reached the front door, a blue light slid out beneath it. As Bernie grasped the knob tightly, she grasped his shoulder tighter. "Do you think we should," she gasped.

"Only one way to find out," he answered before both were blinded by blue light.

Reflection 2
The Known Gods

Slowly, Bernie's eyes adjusted to the fading blue light after a few blinks.

Bernie and Beatrice found themselves in a large room that did not seem to fit into the mansion. The unpainted walls appeared to be stone and were adorned with colorful tapestries. Potted plants filled the chilly room, as did beakers filled with liquids of various hues. The plants' reflections were caught by a large self-standing mirror in the corner of the room. A plush scarlet rug covered the floor and muffled the approach of a statuesque blonde clad in a skimpy evergreen dress that flowed to her bare ankles and was bonded by golden rings at her slender side. Her hair fell over her naked shoulders. Her sparkling green eyes darted from beaker to beaker.

Bernie approached her from behind and wondered aloud, "I wonder if I can touch her?"

"I bet you'd like to," Beatrice sarcastically commented.

Whirling about to face his wife, Bernie gave her a mocking look and then said, "Let's find out."

His hand slowly lifted and Bernie hesitantly tapped the woman on the shoulder.

She spun about. Silently, she brushed her shoulder with her thin fingers. Then she ignored the invisible fingers snapping.

"Your usual reaction from women. I bet that lace wasn't your first choice," Beatrice heckled.

A voice said, "We mustn't risk losing a beauty such as you, Dallyah."

Bernie turned to Beatrice who shrugged and said, "It wasn't me."

A long-haired man in a green robe, which revealed his bare chest, stood in the doorway of a secret passage. His blue eyes brightly glimmered.

Dallyah's attention returned to the beakers and tubes. Finally, she selected one with a lavender liquid. Lifting it to her thin nose, she inhaled deeply. Then her richly red lips twisted to a smile.

"Found the potion for Synthia," she said.

The man with long brown hair stepped closer and reached for Dallyah but she swiftly dodged his touch.

"You are quick," he commented as he grasped his own arms and folded them. "Tell me, are you aware of the danger of your court?"

She lifted the tube of lavender liquid and held it before his eyes. "I must go."

"Beware," he replied. "You may go very far soon."

She bowed and departed. The green-robed high priest then left, leaving the invisible couple alone in the odd room of mysterious elixirs and intricate tapestries.

Swiftly, Dallyah strode down the wide cement corridors. A cold wind whined as it passed through the maze behind her.

A slight press of her hand was all it took for Dallyah to open the large golden door of Belnor's chamber. He lounged on a bed in the center of the room. A single tan sheet entwined his apparently nude muscular body as his damp chest seemed to glisten. His long reddish hair was wet too. As he sat up, he smiled.

"Make your delivery to Synthia?" he asked. His deep voice was friendly.

She nodded and reaching down her side, released the golden rings holding her dress. As the dress fell to the floor, her lips curled quite favorably. Dallyah stepped out of the defeated dress and lunged onto the bed where she embraced Belinor and removed his cover. She licked her lips as she drank in Belinor's body. All senses enjoyed him, from sight to scent.

Then it was his turn.

He gave his eyes a rest and allowed his hands to flow over her body. Her thin yet firm form was pale and smelled of fresh apples. She smiled as his hands reached her hips. Her face fell to his. Their lips met. Other body parts entwined.

Afterward, as the two laid still in bed, staring at the ceiling, Belinor asked, "Have you had an audience with Irlan regarding future commitments?"

"No," Dallyah said softly with an unseen shake of her head.

"You must be careful. That high priest is tricky and dangerous," Belinor sighed before sitting up. He then leaned on his left arm to look into Dallyah's piercing green eyes. "From the way, he looks at you, I'd judge him both attracted and distrustful of you."

Just then, there was a bang at the door and an order. "Open. In the name of Irlan, we are to arrest Belinor and bring forth Dallyah for judging."

Dallyah gasped in horrified shock as both she and her lover leaped from the bed. Her lover grasped the hilt of his sword from the room's bare corner. He lifted it over his head as armed soldiers stormed the room.

The intruders were clad in tin helmets and drab grey tunics. The first thrust his blade at Belinor but ended up with his foe's sword in his gut. But the other soldiers soon flooded over Belinor who was assaulted with pokes by swords before being led away.

Dallyah covered her nudity with her hands as she stood in front of three remaining soldiers.

"We are to take you to Irlan," the first announced after examining her with his eyes.

She at last reached for her fallen dress on the floor. Moving forward, the soldier then stepped on it.

"You are to have no place to hide the workings of a spell," he said.

"Let's go, indecent witch," the other soldier mockingly added before he and his comrade led the devastated blonde out of the room with their firmly held blades. Her naked feet failed to create a patter on the cold stone floor.

Belinor was mocked by soldiers who with firm hands pulled him from darkness into the bright sunlight that fell into a circular arena. His sandaled feet churned through the dust. Clumps of, it marked his passage. Some of it had been stained scarlet by the blood of previous combatants.

A sword was tossed into the warm ring, which Belinor quickly clenched. Through narrowed eyes, he saw Irlan seated at the top deck, framed by barely dressed women. The rumble of voices was lowered as Irlan rose and lifted one hand. "The prize of the contest for the warrior is Belinor's freedom should my champions be defeated."

Irlan dropped his hand and a metal gate whirred open to reveal three men clad in tan loincloths, matching the garment Belinor had been given to wear. Two held swords while the third wielded a mighty mace. All had long hair that hung over muscular shoulders. Each maintained a mean smirk.

Belinor steadied his two-handed grips of the sword and spread his muscular legs to ready his stance for the imminent assault. The mace warrior lunged forward and struck at him with the weapon. Belinor easily avoided the blow and, with his blade, slashed his foe's right ribs. Blood trickled from the wound and the attacker toppled onto the burning sand which quickly adopted a scarlet hue.

The remaining warriors encircled Belinor without stretched swords. A strike at Belinor brought no rewards to save a cut across the chest of the desperately out-numbered warrior. A second attempt resulted in Belinor ducking before crossing blades with his foe. Belinor fell away and found himself on the ground.

Rolling away, a cloud of dust rose. Momentarily, blindness proved long enough for Belinor to rise behind his foe and with the hilt of his sword, strike the back of his opponent's head. The man fell face-first to the ground.

A whip snaked about Belinor's legs and brought him unconscious to the sand.

Irlan stepped forward from his place, face twisted in outrage. He wanted Belinor dead.

"The contest is ended for now," Irlan announced.

As two small men lugged Belinor's heavy body from the ring, the last man standing bowed to Irlan and departed. On his way out, Irlan leaned toward a stooge. "See to it that that one competes in tomorrow's event," Irlan ordered. He then added, "But be sure his whip is taken."

Irlan stood alone in his quarters save for a bird of prey and two invisible watchers. Irlan lifted a hand toward the bird as it sat on the weak limbs of a large plant. In his fingers were small dried beans. The bird took the beans in his beak and began crunching.

"What now?" Beatrice asked over Bernie's shoulder in response to their appearance.

"Shhh," he muttered with a shrug of his shoulders. His attention quickly turned to the nude blonde as she was led in by the soldiers.

"You've always had a thing for blondes, haven't you?" Beatrice pondered aloud to no reply.

"The priestess for your judgment, my lord," the first soldier said as the blonde took her place at the room's center.

"Belinor was given the honor of combat and now dwells as a captive in a cell," Irlan explained.

Dallyah's hands feebly covered her nudity in demanded respect, not embarrassment. She stared forward in defiance, not submission.

Irlan turned before saying, "Excellent. You may go."

"Very good, my lord," said the first man before turning to his fellow soldier. The soldiers bowed before departing.

Irlan now believed himself alone with the nude priestess and stepped toward her. His lips curved in a menacing grin conveying lust. He breathed in deeply and placed his fingers beneath her chin to raise her eyes to stare into his. "I find you most desirable due to your obvious beauty and extensive knowledge of magic," he said gruffly before stepping forward. He lifted a hand to his head. With his fingers, he flicked his long hair aside his face to fully reveal his brown eyes. "Say what you think of me."

"I think you a cruel and loathsome man unfit for the grand office he has attained," she sternly began. "Your post was assumed by bloodletting, deceit, and bribery. You find wicked solace in the cruel punishments this office allows you to oversee."

"Enough," Irlan shouted as he backed away clenching his head in anger and without looking at her, who was to be his victim. He held his stomach with both hands as if punched. "Why do you treat so he with the power to save you?"

"I believe the cost of your price would be too high," she calmly replied.

"Damn you! I wanted to save you," he coldly commented as he spun away from her. "I had hoped to keep you as my woman, but now you shall be banished forever from Atlantis. Never again shall you set foot on this soil."

"I said I feared you set prices too high."

"You have no respect for the Gods!" Irlan bitterly spat at her. "You should never have been given your position."

"I was not given it. I earned it."

"Away!" Irlan roared. As the two soldiers rushed in, he pointed at the nude priestess and added, "Take her!"

"Yes," replied one soldier as he grasped the naked woman's arm and led her from the room.

Irlan straightened up and regained his composure before turning to the remaining guard. A rumbling of the Earth caused the room to quake. Bernie lunged forward to grasp his wife and a small, circular wooden table on which a miniature mirror rested. Holding the table, he maintained his balance as lava squirted into the air.

A moment later, the recovered high priest walked to the window. Glancing out, he saw a serene scene of nature highlighted by birds, before glancing at the remaining frightened guard. "The shaking of the ground means nothing. Tomorrow, with her foul lover, Dallyah will be taken by ship from the island. She shall regret never seeing Atlantis again," Irlan pondered to himself.

Bernie gasped, but as he looked at Beatrice she was replaced by a blue glow.

Reflection 3
Old Joe's Brew

As the blue light faded, Bernie and Beatrice found themselves in a dark wooden room with two small tables and dust-covered furniture. The scratched legs of the table and furniture were wood. Several paintings adorned the wall, a portrait, and two landscapes. One landscape featured autumn leaves. The other highlighted horses. Colorful vases and other trinkets lined one table. The place was filled with spider webs.

Bernie stepped to a window. He drew back a torn, old curtain. He peered out at the peaceful natural setting of trees and bushes outside. It almost matched the painting. Even several horses grazed nearby in a small pen. A breeze ruffled fallen leaves and sent them skimming along the ground.

"Where are we now?" asked Beatrice.

"We could be anywhere," Bernie replied as he watched through a wooden fence a cow graze upon the still lush green grass.

"My bet would be America, the old west," Beatrice said.

"And why guess that?" Bernie asked as he turned.

"Always look to the fashions first," Beatrice replied as she pointed toward the wall hook from which hung a cowboy hat and old denim jacket.

As she walked to the door, Bernie rolled his shoulders and muttered, "Always something to be said for the full-time shopper."

A loud creak sounded as Beatrice opened the wooden door. Bernie followed her out onto the boards of the narrow porch where he found her standing still and watching an Indian fellow seated on an old wooden rocker who strummed a guitar while humming. His thin, chapped lips moved only slightly as his thin fingers nimbly glided across the guitar's strings. He wore an old jacket with cuffs that stretched wide above his wrists and an old brown hat with a wide brim. Long black locks of hair fell beneath it and covered his ears. His skin appeared smooth and untarnished. His dark blue eyes stared down at the instrument he flawlessly played.

As excitement for the music increased, the guitar's head struck an empty bottle on the adjacent round table. The bottle fell without breaking to the porch and rolled to Beatrice's feet. She bent over and picked it up.

"Strong glass," she commented as she tapped it.

She stared at the label. It read OLD JOE'S BREW. Beneath it was listed its miraculous abilities, such as curing coughs and colds. It also granted youthfulness and long life. A primitive drawing of a cactus adorned the label.

"Who is he?" Beatrice said both quietly and calmly.

"How should I know?" Bernie replied.

"I am Old Joe," the stranger said in a deep voice while looking up and placing his guitar on his knee.

"He can see us," Beatrice gasped before turning to Bernie and adding, "How can that be?"

"Don't know and don't know," Bernie answered as he took the bottle from her and looked it over. "This seems to be an old-fashioned elixir such as medicine men used to peddle."

"It is strong medicine. My father's recipe which I successfully sold throughout the valley," Joe replied. "Everyone bought a bottle to use until the local doctor became upset. Thought he was losing business because of it. Claimed I was a fraud and a quack. Called elixir a placebo and a fake. But I always used it and it was good."

Joe rubbed a hand over his face before continuing.

"The doctor formed a mob. Mostly disgruntle businessmen and disappointed farmers who believed my power was disrupting their dreams. He led them to my old house and what started as a gun-waving shoving match ended with a burning."

Beatrice covered her mouth and gasped. Her desire to bury her face at Bernie's shoulder was strong but avoided.

"That night ended with my house reduced to rubble and my wife dead. One shot for me."

Old Joe stood. He took a second to straighten and shake off the day's chill. Then he walked to the edge of the porch and surveyed his land while facing away from his visitors.

"Haven't had a desire to help my fellow man since that night. In the flames, they all looked like demons to me," Joe explained. "I bought this land with elixir money, not buried in the bag, they stole from me that night. Now, I mostly just tend to some animals here and some crops outback. I sometimes make a little elixir just for myself. It keeps me moving. After all, it kept me alive."

Joe removed his hat and put his hands on the back of his head. He parted his thick black hair to reveal a small hole encircled by scabs splattered with blood and emerald ooze.

Beatrice gasped again and this time, she did clutch Bernie and buried her face in his arm to block out the horrific view even as the shimmering blue light enveloped her and her husband. "Do you think it was the elixir that kept him alive that allowed him to see us?" she asked even as they began to disappear.

"Don't have an answer to that or where we're going next."

Reflection 4
A Safe Place

Bernie and Beatrice found themselves in the grey morning hues of an old graveyard. It was empty, saved for one aged man who held a vase of brightly hues flowers. He had short grey hair and a thick mustache of a similar hue. His mud-caked shoes trudged through the muck with squeaky urgency toward a large gravestone that towered in the field's center. Carved into the top of the marble monument were the words – HERE LIES MARY SCMITTER, BELOVED AND CHERISHED WIFE.

Stepping forward, he muttered, "Oh Mary, how I miss you more each day." His long whiskers fluttered from his words. He then placed the vase of flowers upon the grave. Turning, he exhaled and let his shoulders droop from their respectful position. Quietly he walked away.

Beatrice left her husband standing alone in the overgrown grass and scampered toward the old tombstone. She knelt before it and brushed the dust from the carved letters. "Mary Scmitter," she read, "1910 to 1974."

"How sad," he muttered as he watched the figure depart. Turning to his wife, he muttered, "Somehow that name is familiar."

"Doesn't mean a thing to me," Beatrice retorted. "At least he didn't seem to see us."

"No elixir for him, I guess," Bernie replied before approaching the forlorn grave. Staring at it, he added, "Well we've at least reached beyond 1974. Care to make a more accurate prediction, oh great one?"

Stepping forward, Beatrice commented, "Judging from the clothes, I would guess the early eighties."

Soon the graveyard became eerier in the quiet dawn. As the departing figure reached the vanishing point of the lead bars of the cemetery's gate, Beatrice said, "Do you think we should follow him?"

Bernie shook his head. "No, I feel he'll always come back here. I believe he is tied to this spot."

"Poor guy. Just as we are now, thanks to the midnight mansion," Beatrice added.

***

With his beaten feather duster, the old man scattered accumulated dust to the four corners of the antique store's display room. A man clothed in a trench coat with a derby pulled down over his eyes, bent down to peer into display cases with surprisingly shiny glass.

"Looking for anything in particular? We have a wide range of items. We have watches, books, and coins. One coin is imbued with magic if you believe the stories. I am the store's owner, Michael Maine."

"Do not worry or trouble yourself," the visitor said as he straightened and turned from the glass. "I seek you."

Michael shot him a disturbingly worried look.

"Or perhaps I should say I seek Michael Scmitter."

At the name, the old man slumped down behind the large front desk upon which sat old earrings, cuff links, old coins, and necklaces as well as chains. He collapsed into a chair which creaked as he adjusted his position.

"How did you find me?" Michael inquired as he ran a withered hand through thinning hair.

"I am most persistent and not put off or phased by a name change."

"It would have been in another section of the phone book."

The stranger let out a laugh.

"From this place, I see you have done very well for yourself since the war," the visitor said as he revealed a bald head once the derby was removed for fanning purposes. Michael took a coin from its box and let it shift over his fingers.

"I did." The old man gazed up into the stranger's unmoving beady eyes magnified by glasses. "And for my wife."

"Ach, yes of course," the stranger quickly replied. "She was taken by cancer."

Michael nodded, maintaining a silently chilling stare at the stranger.

"Well, I shall simply state the purpose for my visit."

"Please do."

"I want money. The tale is you escaped from Germany after the war with a large amount of it."

The stranger removed a handkerchief from his pocket. Then took off his damp spectacles and wiped them. "A thousand dollars should do well. That shall ensure my silence in regard to your identity."

"For now?" Michael asked.

The stranger let out a laugh before sounding the bell above the front door and promising to return the next day. He didn't even bother to look at the crumpled old man who sat tiredly with his head in his hands. All he could do was summon up memories of his past with Mary in Germany as he repeatedly muttered her name.

Thus he sat long into the night until he summoned the energy to stand. He grabbed his tattered coat. It was not nearly as impressive as his finely tailored officer uniform jacket had been, that fit sharply while carrying an edge with its dark hue and sparkling gold chest medals. Michael slipped the old coin into his pocket and strode out into the night's swirling wind.

At the end of his walk, Michael's tired legs found him at his wife's grave. He didn't notice the lingering invisible eyes of Bernie and Beatrice that watched him as he toppled before the tombstone. He clutched the cold stone.

"Mary," he muttered again. The name gave him peace but failed to slow his rapid heart rate. He tugged his handkerchief from his pocket and blew his nose before wiping tears from his eyes. "If only I could be with you again. Forget all this," Michael practically moaned from the grave.

His hand found the old coin in his pocket. For a brief second, he believed he saw it glow. But then thought it must be a trick of the moonlight.

"I wish I could just find a safe place," Michael sobbed pathetically as he punched the gravestone until his knuckles bled. Finally, his bloody hand opened and the coin fell to the earth. "Mary, I want to be with you again – forever."

At that, Michael collapsed beneath the tombstone and lay unmoving.

Michael inhaled stale air. There was a wretched scent present which Michael could not accurately describe.

Michael's eyes fluttered open but did not find the light. He tried to rise from where he lay but struck his head against something hard. He exclaimed a stream of profanity. Lifting his arms, his hands pressed against the barrier above. As his one hand fell, it landed on top of a body next to him.

The body was cold and hard. Finally, Michael found a match in his pocket. He lit it and brought it before the body next to him. The woman wore a familiar silver dress. It was the dress his wife had been buried in.

Michael screamed.

The cry echoed beyond the grave.

"What's that?" Beatrice said as she turned from Bernie toward the grave.

A blue light consumed the grave before taking Beatrice and Bernie.

Reflection 5
Severe Secrets

Tiff removed her dress and stepped into the shower. The water was warm. A soft sigh resulted from her lips at first contact with the exhilarating drops.

The young lady failed to reach the height of five feet and was somewhat stocky, but she had beautiful curves. Her body had often proved quite kissable. Everywhere.

The shower suddenly stopped of its own accord.

The once white wall was splattered with dirt and grime. Her long brown hair was tied into a ponytail. She gave the shower's tarnished silver handle a twist to which she only got a loud knocking sound in reply instead of the water's return. "Really," she muttered aloud disgustedly to herself. She fiddled with the control and finally as a reward received a warm downpour.

She unwrapped a small bar of yellow soap. Tossing away the paper wrapper, she began to lather up. First, her hands and then her legs were covered with lather and bubbles. She smiled at a certain naughty satisfaction achieved at washing below her waist and then her chest.

Engrossed with the shower, she failed to hear the door to the motel room open or approaching footsteps followed by a creak of the bed.

Wet and renewed, Tiff stepped from the shower and grabbed the old towel which hung nearby. It was white with green trim.

The towel was not as thick and fluffy as Tiff would have liked. Plus it was a bit too small, encouraging a fight as she attempted to slip it around herself. "Damn," Tiff muttered upon noticing several rips and holes in the old towel which adorned her. Tiff sighed before departing the bathroom for the outer room.

There, she found Ethan on the bed waiting for her, shirt and shoes removed. "You look great," he commented leaning forward with a smile.

"It has holes in it," she dejectedly said.

"I just wish they were bigger," he laughed. "After all, I didn't come here to see a towel. I came to see you. Take it off."

At first, she sighed at his suggestion. Then she grinned before the revelation of her beautiful bare body as she tossed aside the towel and giggled. Her skin was unblemished and a thick growth of hair covered her twat.

"Like it?" she asked, hand on hip and legs slightly spread.

Ethan's eyes widened as he nodded before stretching his open arms toward her. She accepted his embrace as she crawled into bed on top of him. Their lips met for a kiss. Once on top of him, there was a large bulge beneath his pants poking between her legs. She did not pause, only smiled before licking her lips and finding a job for her mouth on his face.

He laid back in bed and listened to the sound of his zipper open. A second later, he felt her warm fingers fish his cock out of his pants. He closed his eyes, smiling, as he felt his penis in her mouth.

He opened his eyes and peered at the large circular mirror that stood courtesy of a metal stand across from them. He stared at the glorious view of her ass it provided as her mouth worked its magic on his throbbing erection.

Then the view seemed to change with a scarlet shimmer. An ass was still there, but it was rounder and tanner, belonging to a raven-haired beauty who committed the same act on a different man. The woman happily laughed as the man rubbed her back and switched position. Now facing her bottom, he reached for her shapely cheeks and spread them. His mouth drew closer in order to kiss his chosen target.

As Ethan watched, his erection grew thanks both to Tiff's attention and the entertainment he viewed.

The man in the mirror had abandoned kissing his girl's ass and moved his cock into position behind her asshole. He quietly plunged it in her. Her reaction was not quiet at all, in tune with the outrageous wide-eyed look on her face. As Ethan watched the action, he felt himself grow harder in Tiff's mouth. Then the lady relaxed, smiling slightly at the man's anal intrusion. His hands found her shoulders to massage, as he continued to enjoy her from the inside out.

After he came tremendously, he heard a gulping sound from Tiff. Her mouth released his still massive and twitching cock, leaving him wanting more.

Without asking, he knelt behind her and got a grip on her ample hips which he brought upward. A second and mighty push later, he was in her ass. She finally sighed as she felt his cum pour within her. He withdrew. She silently walked away. He turned to gaze at her to witness the movement of her every muscle as she departed. Especially her cute ass.

"Something new," she said as she selected an old washrag and tossed it to him. "I approve."

"Good," he yawned as he stretched.

"Clean yourself up," she suggested. "No one likes a dirty cock. Be sure to have my ass scent off before you return to your wife."

As he proceeded to wipe his cock with the moist washrag, he rose from the bed and approached the mirror. Bending forward, nothing revealed itself in the glass save the dirty room they had entered. Spiders crawled across the web-covered glass. The spiders ignored their webs once noticing they were vacant of prey. Ethan stood up straight, his enlarged cock wagging only for the invisible guests to see.

Ethan scampered into the drug store where Tiff manned a rusted old cash register. He approached her at the counter and asked, "Tomorrow night at eight good for you?"

"Sure," she replied with an enthusiastic nod that propelled her long bangs over her eyes. "We could enjoy ourselves most of the night. My old man doesn't get home till late. Same place?"

Ethan nodded. "I enjoyed the entertainment there."

Tiff nodded, not realizing the full connotation of what he referred to.

When the two illicit lovers found themselves back at the same hotel, they again entered the familiar dust-strewn room. Ethen followed Tiff, ogling her, and she tossed aside her oversize football sweatshirt and then unzipped her bright red mini-skirt. She showed no shyness in the sudden revelation of her pink panties. With a tired groan born of a long day at work, she kicked off her heels. She propped her bare arms up over the churning air conditioner. Her moist underarms soaked up the cool air. Then as one hand fell to the panty band at her thigh, she immodestly asked, "You ready for this?"

Ethan only nodded. She then rapidly removed her panties. She stood nude before him only wearing a wicked smile. Her lips twitched as she heavily breathed. "Ready to be fucked, big boy?" She said before jumping forward toward him, rushing him back toward the bed as he removed his garments.

As she lay atop him, his erection indicated his excitement even as he stared over her shoulder at the mirror. "The actions here," she commented as she pinched her hard nipples to prove a point. They were pale red petals ready for plucking, and his tongue hungrily did so as his dick poked her harder between the legs. She sighed before grinding her body into his. She felt him throb in excitement.

Then there was his voice, "Do you ever see a strange colored mist flowing from the mirror? Or strangers in it?"

"No. Why?" she said, before ignoring his quiet response. Then in an assumed sexy voice, she added, "Just you and me in it, big boy." She took his head in her hands. She placed it between her legs and playfully 'slapped' the sides of his head with her inner thighs.

He crawled up her and his gaze returned to her eyes as her tongue played with his manhood. He closed his eyes and smiled in reaction to her attention. When again opened, his eyes witnessed the scarlet glow emanate from the mirror to fill the room. Now as he stared into the mirror, he saw himself replaced by a mustached muscleman who kissed the flat stomach of an ebony beauty beneath him. Her luxurious long hair flowered over the pillows and her smile grew as his lips lowered. Firmly, he spread her thin legs, first for his mouth and then for his cock. Her head reared back as she scratched his back. In response to the action and knowing what was to come next, both smiled. He entered her.

As the activity reached its end, Ethan's attention returned to Tiff. He kissed her and let a wondering hand explore the beautiful feminine territory between her legs. His lips attacked her neck. She sighed as his hardened cock entered her. The event ended quickly leaving both satisfied and the mirror merely depicting a room empty, safe for the tired couple cuddling on the bed.

The next day, Ethan returned alone to the rundown motel. Entering the front room, he was greeted by the familiar face of pimples belonging to the bald and overweight manager. The young man was attired in loosely fitting old clothes. "Here again? Need a room?"

Ethan ignored the first question and shook his head at the second.

"Have you noticed anything strange going on here?"

"Dude, this is a cheap 70 bucks a night hotel in the middle of nowhere. Everything going on here is strange." The manager grabbed a few loose papers from the scratched and marked desk to shuffle through. From his pocket, he produced a candy bar and with his teeth tore the package open.

"Any odd sightings in the rooms? Weird ghost-like appearances?"

"A few weird sightings but no ghosts. They're too straight-laced for this place. No ghost vacancies available."

"Any strangers wondering about?"

"This is a motel, remember? Everyone wondering about is a stranger."

"Thanks for the help," Ethan sighed as he turned to leave. He opened the door and stuck a foot out.

"See ya next time ya need a room," the motel clerk called after him. "Remember, we've the best room rate in town."

***

The motel clerk hid any surprise at Ethan's return a few nights later as he simply pulled a key from its place and exchanged it for the bills in Ethan's hand. Upon examining the key, Ethan noticed a different number.

"I want the usual room, not this one," Ethan said.

"They're all the same," the manager tiredly groaned.

"Okay. I'll hold you to it," Ethan joked as he thumbed the key before turning and departing.

Ethan hoped into his car beside the vivaciously dressed Tiff and pulled the vehicle around back. When it came to a halt before a different room, Tiff commented, "New room?"

"None of the rooms here are new," Ethan said before following her in where she removed her clothes and headed to the bed as he moved the stand of a mirror in the room's corner to a position directly before the bed.

"What are you doing?" Tiff inquired.

Ethan ignored her and upon completing the task, started to remove his clothes. He jumped in bed with Tiff, but it was the mirror that commanded his attention. He saw himself pose his cock straight up in the glass. Finally, he saw Tiff lean toward his crotch, but no one appeared in the mirror as she sucked him.

He enjoyed their exchanges. Kisses, caresses, and more. He came in her soft mouth. Yet somehow, he was disappointed. And the mirror remained barren of all but their reflection.

"They didn't come," he muttered, a blank stare on his face.

"Relax. You did," she replied mischievously with a naughty smile as she stroke her leg.

Ethan turned to her, a wild look in his eye that didn't disappear with a kiss.

***

Once again Ethan returned to the dilapidated motel. Once again the manager waited at the desk. This time as the manager slid the key across the desk, Ethan halted it with one hand and said, "I want the first room I rented again."

"Did the last room disappoint you?"

"A bit," Ethan tersely answered with tight lips. He sent the offered key back at the manager and smiled when his hand again clutched the familiar key of the other stay. Room nine, it said.

93

Ethan returned to his car where Tiff waited wearing a blue blouse and denim skirt which he reached beneath for play. She purred approvingly. "I'll take that to mean you're ready." He took his hand from her to the wheel. A second later, they were parked back in front of good old room number nine.

He followed her into the room where it was slightly hotter than it was outside. She checked the air unit and quickly removed her top, revealing she was bra-less before her hands moved to the belt on her skirt. It was quickly dealt with as well. She was tan from the last sunbath of summer. Her legs may be somewhat short but she knew how to use them.

Soon the cool breezes of autumn would arrive, bringing hay, colorful leaves, and ghosts. The final fall thought brought the mirror to Ethan's mind. He turned to it. Scrutinizing the glass revealed no images save for himself and Tiff. She reached for her panties and removed them. The action induced a stiffness that revealed itself as Ethan energetically stepped out of his pants and took Tiff in his bare arms.

With one eye, Ethan peered at the newly formed mist and unfamiliar bodies that appeared in the mirror. An older man with thinning grey hair watched two nude women frolic playfully onto the bed. The taller female was blonde with big breasts. The shorter girl had long, dark hair. She reminded Ethan of Tiff, who would soon be under him. The two women giggled as the brunette parted her legs for the blonde, who greedily kissed the offered area before rubbing her pussy and holding her hand up to be stroked by the other's tongue.

The scene unleashed Ethan's excitement so that he flipped Tiff over and spanked her bare ass. He had done this action accidentally once before and Tiff's moans were arousing. He buried his face in the warm flesh of her ass cheeks. He deeply filled his lungs with her scent. It was earthy. Certainly sexy. Definitely her. His tongue tasted her. Tiff turned over and mounted her lover. As her moans grew louder, his climax neared.

Moonlight washed over the two tired lovers as they traipsed out to Ethan's car. "It's still hot."

"It sure is," Ethan added with a chuckle.

"Same time next week good for you?"

"Yep."

"Wanna try someplace new? Maybe the swanky hotel downtown?" Tiff asked, looking away from the moon.

"No," Ethan said as he turned to her and switched on the ignition. His gaze returned to the pavement as his tire busted a bottle and flattened a soda can abandoned in the parking lot.

****

The day was fading when Ethan's car unleashed a cloud of dust and gravel in Tiff's narrow dirt driveway. Ethan exited the car and slammed the door. As he approached the screen door, Tiff approached its window and softly said, "It's over."

"What? Is this because of how I acted in the room?"

Tiff vehemently shook her head, causing several bangs to descend over her eyes. Ethan noticed a puffy black mark near her left eye. "He knows about us."

She then moved back, disappearing within to be replaced by a large man clad in a dark t-shirt and blue shorts. He had receding brown hair and eyes matching the color of the shorts. A goatee hung from his chin.

Stepping to the door, the man opened it. "How's the computer biz going?"

"Usual," Ethan lightly replied. "Things at the garage?"

"Same. Beer?"

"No thanks." Ethan assumed an air of comfort on the porch before fidgeting began.

"I think I'll forget the time and get one. Anything I can do for you?"

Ethan shook his head.

"I am going to get that beer. See you later?"

Ethan remained speechless as the wood door slammed shut. He turned. Before descending the porch, he thought he heard a strike.

***

A different clerk was watching over the broken-down motel's front desk a month later one afternoon. It was a middle-aged man with beady brown eyes. He had no hair on top of his head but made up for it beneath his chin.

Ethan had decided to depart work early after lunch. Business at the programing center was slow, which bored Ethan. His thoughts turned to the opposite gender and he thought he might find the beautiful image of one to gaze at, preferably with his hand in his pants attending to carnal need.

Upon Ethan's request for a room, the motel employee reached for a key but Ethan asked for room nine. With a strange look, the bearded man produced the appropriate key for Ethan, who left humming.

Ethan entered room nine, remembering his strange experiences there with Tiff. He immediately unzipped his pants. Clothes were quickly removed until he found himself nude. Before the mirror, his hand gently ran over his torso before it lowered to his cock to commence preening. Taking the limp organ between his fingers, he stretched it out then settled onto the bed. His shaft towered between his legs. He stared at the mirror…waiting.

Nothing.

Only the image of his frenzied masturbation inhabited the mirror.

***

Several days passed without a word from Tiff. Ethan tried calling her a few times. Either her husband answered or her voice was replaced by silence followed by a decisive click.

Ethan decided to alter his approach. The bell above the drug store heralded his arrival with a ring. Neither it nor his presence had much of an effect on Tiff as she stood by the register vacantly looking at a magazine. A bored look etched on her practically comatose face.

Ethan plopped his hands on the counter. "Hi, honey."

"What can I do for you?" Tiff coldly asked while not bothering to look him in the eye.

"Why've you been a stranger? Hubby giving you trouble? A pounding, perhaps?"

"Not surprisingly, he's acting like a Neanderthal," Tiff replied while turning her attentive eyes to his. "And you…you've just been acting so weird. What's gotten into you? Or should I ask what have you gotten into?"

"Look baby, I'm sorry hubby is giving you trouble, but it shouldn't affect us."

"Well, what is there to us aside from an occasional fuck? And now that just gets you weird."

"No…"

"Get out," she screamed. A toss of her magazine had it reaching the door before him.

***

Bored, horny, and ready, Ethan decided to proceed with a solo performance. He stroked and fondled the entirety of his shaft as he lay nude upon the bed of room nine.

Closing his eyes, he allowed a dozen images to run through his mind as he slowly stroked his cock. His closed eyes tightened as thoughts of beautiful bodies held sway. Memories of past times were included as well as strictly fantasies. He felt twitches as his penis hardened while lengthening at the thought of kissing the lithe bodies upon areas usually hidden by garments.

Remembrances of warm lips intimately connecting with his body brought his arousal to staggering proportions. His eyes lazily opened to look down at himself. But it was the mist enshrouding the mirror that caught his attention.

Without releasing his cock, he sat up. As he neared the mirror, the forms present there in the glass became clearer. A young big breasted brunette dived at the crotch of a portly man with curly hair. Both were naked. As she lapped his nether region, he smiled and patted her head while cooing. He twisted her hair around his fat fingers and brought her face up to his. He belched a comment into her ear. Then he stuck his tongue into her mouth.

As he did so, Ethan felt himself throb. His eyes became heavy even as his addiction to watching grew. The heavy man grabbed the girl's ankles and spread her legs. Ready or not, willing or not, she was invaded by his stiffness. She cried and Ethan did as well as she when she came.

Ethan ran a hand over his forehead. It was moist. He found his chest so as well when he ran a hand over it. But the wettest area was most assuredly between his legs. At the first few steps, he realized his legs were weak.

Then he realized he had just as much fun alone as with Tiff.

Thus, he was influenced to travel alone to the motel each night where he discovered the bald manager hunched over a small table boasting a men's magazine and a paper plate with cooling slices of pizza. Upon seeing him, the manager would smile and grab key number nine to slide to him with the wish, "Hope you have a good evening, sir."

Without pausing to administer a greeting, Ethan would take the key, leave behind the appropriate amount of cash crumpled up on the desk, and turn toward the door. He then strode to his car, ignoring all sirens, screeching tires, or other sounds of the city that he heard.

In a flash, he would be back in room nine. Quickly he'd discard his clothes and adopt his position on the bed, eyes concentrating on the mirror as hands expertly sought out appropriate positions on his body to enjoy the ensuing tableau on the mirror. Women and men of all nationalities and ages assembled to engage in carnal delights.

Then one morning, Ethan never returned with his key to the front office. The morning clerk was mystified to not encounter his friend, but concerned would be too strong a word. He stroked a thin hand over his unshaved wide chin. Then with the master key, he went to room nine.

Two raps on the door brought no response. Finally, the master key was called into use. With a creek, the door was slowly opened. The room was a dirty shambles. Therefore nothing was unusual.

"Hello, anyone here?" the clerk called out as he entered the room, failing to note the strange mist enshrouding the floor. All seemed normal as the clerk shrugged and headed for the door.

Only the invisible Bernie and Beatrice saw Ethan trapped within the mirror. He put his hands to the glass at first, but escape was impossible. Beating his hands against the inside of the glass also proved an impossible escape effort. Finally, he settled on the bed and did what came naturally for any able to watch.

Ethan came.

Reflection 6
Endgame

Bernie and Beatrice exchanged confused looks as they stared into the mirror at Ethan.

"Are you okay?" Bernie asked as he turned toward his wife.

"Better than him," Beatrice answered while pumping her thumb at the mirror.

"Good point," Bernie answered more loudly while straightening. As if for the first time, he acted confidently that they could not be seen.

"What now?" Beatrice confusedly wondered.

They both just silently stared at the mirror until she pondered, "You think he can get out of there?"

"Don't know. But mirrors have been in the old midnight house as well as the time streams we've visited," Bernie realized aloud.

"Do you think we could travel through them?" Beatrice wondered aloud. "Get back?"

"To the old mansion? Well, mirrors do supposedly have magical properties," Bernie replied while rubbing his chin and staring at the mirror. "After all, they were unable to capture the supernatural image of vampires. They've had a history of being used by magicians and have been at all the places we've visited."

"But how do we get in them?" Beatrice marveled as she stood back.

"I doubt a running start will help," Bernie replied as he cautiously stretched out his hands toward the mirror.

Ethan remained ignorant of the actions as he continued his own motions. Bernie found the glass cool to the touch of his pressed hands. But as he exerted pressure, a tingling sensation enveloped in his fingers. He heard Beatrice call out his name as his person transferred to the other side of the glass.

Beatrice confusedly approached him as he stared out at her from the other side of the mirror's reflective surface. He didn't hear her but saw his name voiced via her mouth. Excitedly with waving hands, he urged her to step forward and touch the glass. Bernie let out a sigh as she did so, and within a second she could hear his heavy breathing. She was on the other side. Turning to him she gasped.

Looking at Ethan, she rolled her eyes and noted he was too concerned with his own matters to care about her activity. She felt Bernie touch her arm and pull her toward him. Then they were moving, somehow racing from mirror environment to mirror environment. After the old motel room, she found herself traveling through the antique shop. Then it was Old Joe's room that she was in. Suddenly, she was traveling back to Atlantis. Then, finally, she was surrounded by the gloom of the midnight mansion as a full moon hovered outside a window.

Smiling with stunned satisfaction as she gazed at the room's dusty environment, she hugged Bernie as she muttered, "We've done it. We're back!"

Bernie kissed her and momentarily returned the affection of her hug before releasing her and stepping away.

"Now what?" she asked while closely watching his movements.

"We find Charlton and our son," he said as he moved off through the room without looking at her.

"In that order?" she wondered while glancing at the fireplace's fan of flame and running a hand through her hair.

"Not necessarily," was his curt reply. "First we prepare." He stepped toward a large, dust-covered metal cabinet and reached for a knob on its door. Opening it, his eyes grew at the sight of guns stacked on a rack within. He reached in and selected a handgun. The weapon felt good in his grasp, reminding him of his old days in the army. A quick opening of the gun revealed in its interior silver bullets.

"These should do," Bernie commented as he returned the weapon to its working order. A further inspection of the cabinet revealed a small box of silver bullets, which Bernie grasped and slipped into one of his pockets.

Turning to his wife, he asked, "Ready to go?"

She remained both quiet and unmoving before a jewelry box that displayed rings, necklaces, and earrings made with crystals that glowed and sparkled in the dim light from the overhead chandelier of electric lights made to resemble candles. Slowly, she raised a hand and reached forward to touch a necklace's crystal.

"Don't," warned Bernie as her finger neared the crystal.

Ignoring his comment, she touched the crystal, and instantly her eyes slid back as odd images of alien warships and a strange world filled her mind. She screamed.

Bernie raced forward and took her limp body in his arms. Her sighs were replaced by heavy breathing as she settled against him.

"Are you okay?"

"I guess so," she replied, her eyes fixed on the jewelry box. "I just got such a strange taste of power from those things plus odd memories of another place and time."

"Not surprising, I suppose," Bernie commented as he helped Beatrice from the room after checking that the gun was secure at the back of his belt.

***

Bernie opened the next door they came to and joined his wife in a gasp of horror. Upon the floor lay the practically decapitated body of Mrs. Millstream like a broken doll, while her child hung lifeless from a noose above.

Bernie slammed shut the door. Turning to his wife, he suggested, "Maybe we should forget about checking any further rooms and just seek who we're looking for."

"I agree."

***

A rumbling sound started outside as storm clouds gathered. Soon the patter of raindrops began their assault upon the midnight mansion's old roof shingles which grew slicker even as Rickie found himself upon them. His flight for escape had brought him to the mansion's highest point, yet Chuckie's pursuit continued.

Due to the weather, the chubby child abandoned his lighter as an instrument of intimidation in favor of the blade he skillfully manipulated in hand. Malevolent chuckles gurgled from his mouth as he neared his feeble prey, who kept losing his footing on the slick roof. Finally, Rickie lost his balance and fell as several shingles, desperately.

The boy's arms stretched out as he flattened against the roof.

Without wasting time, Chuckie was on top of Rickie, knee in the back while blade point rested at the nape of his neck. The wind's growl grew as Chuckie glanced over his shoulder to see Carlton traipsing across the roof. His walking stick was shakily clasped in one hand and his black cloak billowed behind him giving the impression of a mighty bat wing.

"Good work, my boy," Carlton called. He got a mouthful of water as his glasses were pelted by drops of rain. "Finish him off."

Chuckie crafted a ghoulish smirk as he tossed away his soaked paper hat and lifted the blade high overhead where it glittered in the moonlight. Exhausted, Rickie didn't bother to turn over to look back for a face full of rain.

The harsh rain blurred Chuckie's vision as he looked around in time to receive a slap across the face. He staggered back. A fall landed him on his bottom and he looked up to see Beatrice crouched over him.

"You beastly boy! If you ever trouble my son again, I'll do worse."

Chuckie silently looked up from where he lay. He had no desire to tangle again with the hellcat crouched before him. He saw Rickie still strewn across the roof on his front but now face up. Behind him stood Carlton. As Carlton turned to run, he found himself blocked by Bernie. Bernie's face bordered on the grim.

"Well, fancy meeting you here," Carlton feebly quipped.

Without humor, Bernie reached out and clutched Carlton's shirt collar before releasing a powerful blow to the jaw.

Before falling, Carlton's locks of hair shook. The walking stick was released and fell to the roof shingles with a clatter seconds before its owner did.

Bernie then carefully crossed to his wife, with whom he exchanged a hug before kneeling next to his son. "You okay?"

A nod was accepted. Bernie then helped the boy up.

Chuckie scrambled to his feet and allowed the rain to cover his awkward descent from the roof. Beatrice was about to pursue the boy when she felt Bernie's chilly hand on her arm. "Let him go."

"But he should be punished," she said.

"What's the use? I think he has been through enough. Where's he to go?"

Bernie put his arm around his wife. "Let's get some rope to tie Carlton up. Him I have some questions for."

Reflection 7
Explanation and Revelation

What brought Carlton back to consciousness is unknown. Possibly it was being pelted by the rain or dragged downstairs from the roof to an almost empty large room found. Or the murmur of those that encircled him.

Surrounding the fallen Carlton stood Bernie, Beatrice, and Rickie. Slowly, the aged magician made it to his knees, his hands still bound.

There was a steely glint in Bernie's eyes as he raised the gun with silver bullets until its muzzle touched Carlton's forehead.

"What happened to Rachel Millstream?" Bernie inquired while holding the gun firmly.

The old magician ignored the beads of sweat that sprouted from his forehead at the weapon's cold touch and looked up. His eyes raised to meet Bernie's before his dry lips twisted menacingly apart. "She was helpful, in her way," he said while looking up into the darkness of the barrel. His lips twitched into a slight smile of malevolence. "Her purpose ended. I disposed of her easily."

"What was her purpose?!" Bernie demanded, trembling slightly but keeping a still hand.

"To prepare Beatrice and great you all."

Beatrice pulled her son close and engulfed him in a hug which he silently accepted as his eyes fell to the floor.

"Your guilt is found not only by those assembled here but by victims throughout time," Bernie said as his grip on the trigger tightened.

"Go ahead," goaded Carlton, the focus of his grim eyes unchanging. "End it."

Bernie pulled the trigger.

A blast did.

Bernie silently watched Carlton drop to the floor. Blood formed a pool at the magician's head. Bernie turned to his family. Silently, he embraced them, gun still smoking in his hand.

"How do we leave this place now?" Beatrice asked as she stared at Bernie whose face was etched with exhaustion.

Bernie took a deep breath and exchanged looks with his wife before his vision settled on his son.

"We just go," Bernie calmly concluded with a stern statement. "We leave the body and give this place back to the woods."

He embraced his wife and gave her a long kiss.

As he moved away from her, she spoke. "This time, do you think we'll last?"

"We'd better," was his answer as he took his son's hand and started to the door with his family. "After all, if we can survive time trips, won't family vacations be easy?"

The door slammed shut behind him, bringing quiet to the midnight mansion.

***

Sunlight filtered through the green leaves of ancient trees reaching for the blue of the sky. A new day began as a young boy sat at the base of a gnarled old oak tree. His eyes were wet and red from tears.

As he wiped his bruised face, he heard his sobbing outmatched by approaching footsteps and a cane.

"Are you okay, sonny?" asked the tall man who clutched the cane. His long blonde hair fluttered in the breeze.

The young boy inhaled deeply. The effort both brought the boy air and ended his tearful condition. Finally, the boy nodded. "Just a bunch of bully boys," he commented.

"Well they always have been and always will be," the stranger commented before holding out his hand. "Come with me and I'll show you a new way."

Silently the boy stared up at the stranger, whose unmoving hand waited. Finally, he lifted his hand and felt Carlton's cold grip.